FRIENDS OF ACPL

WHERE'S RUFUS?
To librarians, parents, and teachers:

Where's Rufus? is a Parents Magazine READ ALOUD Original — one title in a series of colorfully illustrated and fun-to-read stories that young readers will be sure to come back to time and time again.

Now, in this special school and library edition of *Where's Rufus?,* adults have an even greater opportunity to increase children's responsiveness to reading and learning — and to have fun every step of the way.

When you finish this story, check the special section at the back of the book. There you will find games, projects, things to talk about, and other educational activities designed to make reading enjoyable by giving children and adults a chance to play together, work together, and talk over the story they have just read.

For a free color catalog describing Gareth Stevens' list of high-quality books, call 1-800-341-3569 (USA) or 1-800-461-9120 (Canada).

Parents Magazine READ ALOUD Originals:

Golly Gump Swallowed a Fly
The Housekeeper's Dog
Who Put the Pepper in the Pot?
Those Terrible Toy-Breakers
The Ghost in Dobbs Diner
The Biggest Shadow in the Zoo
The Old Man and the Afternoon Cat
Septimus Bean and His Amazing Machine
Sherlock Chick's First Case
A Garden for Miss Mouse
Witches Four
Bread and Honey
Pigs in the House
Milk and Cookies
But No Elephants
No Carrots for Harry!
Snow Lion
Henry's Awful Mistake
The Fox with Cold Feet
Get Well, Clown-Arounds!
Pets I Wouldn't Pick
Sherlock Chick and the Giant
    Egg Mystery
Cats! Cats! Cats!

Henry's Important Date
Elephant Goes to School
Rabbit's New Rug
Sand Cake
Socks for Supper
The Clown-Arounds Go on Vacation
The Little Witch Sisters
The Very Bumpy Bus Ride
Henry Babysits
There's No Place Like Home
Up Goes Mr. Downs
Bicycle Bear
Sweet Dreams, Clown-Arounds!
The Man Who Cooked for Himself
Where's Rufus?
The Giggle Book
Pickle Things
Oh, So Silly!
The Peace-and-Quiet Diner
Ten Furry Monsters
One Little Monkey
The Silly Tail Book
Aren't You Forgetting Something, Fiona?

Library of Congress Cataloging-in-Publication Data

Calmenson, Stephanie.
    Where's Rufus? / by Stephanie Calmenson; pictures by Maxie Chambliss.
        p. cm. -- (Parents magazine read aloud original)
    "North American library edition"--T.p. verso.
    Summary: The reader tries to find Rufus the dog as he hides in various parts of the house trying to delay the family picnic because he knows it is going to rain.
    ISBN 0-8368-0990-4
    [1. Dogs--Fiction. 2. Picnicking--Fiction. 3. Picture puzzles.] I. Chambliss, Maxie, ill. II. Title. II. Series.
PZ7.C136Wi   1994
[E]--dc20   93-21200

This North American library edition published in 1994 by Gareth Stevens Publishing, 1555 North RiverCenter Drive, Suite 201, Milwaukee, Wisconsin 53212, USA, under an arrangement with Parents Magazine Press, New York.

Printed in the United States of America

1 2 3 4 5 6 7 8 9 99 98 97 96 95 94

Where's Rufus?

A Parents Magazine
Read Aloud Original

Where's Rufus?

by Stephanie Calmenson
pictures by Maxie Chambliss

Gareth Stevens Publishing   •   Milwaukee

Parents Magazine Press   •   New York

To Anthony and Paul Johnson—S.C.

For Michelle and Matt Hoey
with love and dog biscuits—M.C.

"Rise and shine!" said Mr. Plinkett.
"The sun is shining.
It is a perfect day for a picnic."
"Hurray!" said Lucy and Sam.
"Ga, ga," said Baby.
"Woof!" said Rufus.

11

At breakfast, the Plinketts
planned what they would bring.
"Peanut butter and jelly
sandwiches," said Sam.
"Fizzy-Fizz to drink," said Lucy.

While they were talking,
Rufus was looking out the window.
He saw a small, gray rain cloud.
He wanted to tell
the Plinketts about it.

"Woof!" barked Rufus.
"Hush, Rufus," said Mrs. Plinkett.
"We can't think with so much noise."

But Rufus saw another
rain cloud rolling in.
"Woof! Woof!" he barked,
louder than before.
"Down, boy," said Mr. Plinkett.

When Rufus saw one more rain cloud,
he knew it was *not*
a good time for a picnic.

"Www-oof! Www-oof!" howled Rufus.
But he could not get
the Plinketts to turn around.

After breakfast, when Mr. and Mrs. Plinkett
were filling the food basket,
Rufus tried to stop them.

And when Lucy and Sam
were packing their toys,
Rufus tried to take the toys away.

Finally, the Plinketts were ready to go.
Rufus had to think of a new way
to keep them inside.
So, he hid.
"Here, Rufus," called Lucy.
But Rufus didn't come.
"Rufus!" called Sam. "It's time to go."
"Maybe we should leave without him,"
said Mr. Plinkett.
"NO!" cried Lucy and Sam.
"A picnic without Rufus
would be no fun at all!"
Rufus was happy to hear that.

Sam went to the living room
to look for Rufus.
He looked behind the bookcase.
He looked under the couch.
He looked behind the curtains.
But he didn't find Rufus.

Do you know where Rufus is?

25

Rufus raced into the kitchen.
Lucy went there to look for him.
She looked under the table.
She looked in the closet.
She even looked in the refrigerator.
But she didn't find Rufus.

Do you know where Rufus is?

Rufus got to the bathroom
just in time to hide.
Mrs. Plinkett looked behind the door.
She looked in the bathtub.
She looked under the sink.
But she didn't find Rufus.

Do you know where Rufus is?

29

Mr. Plinkett went into the den.
He looked under the desk.
He looked behind the television.
He looked behind the chair.
But he didn't find Rufus.

Do you know where Rufus is?

On the way to Baby's room,
Rufus passed a window and
looked outside.
"Someday they will thank me
for this," he thought.

Baby toddled into her room.
She looked under her crib.
She looked into her toy box.
She looked behind her giraffe.
But she didn't find Rufus.

Do you know where Rufus is?

Suddenly, there was
a crash of thunder.
Rufus jumped into Baby's arms.
"Doggie!" said Baby.

"Good for you, Baby!" said Lucy.
"You found Rufus!"
"Wow! Look at all that rain!" said Sam,
pointing out the window.

40

The Plinketts waited
for the rain to stop.
When the sun was shining again,
they went on their picnic.

"It's a good thing we didn't leave
when we planned," said Mr. Plinkett.
"We can thank Rufus for that,"
said Lucy.

"Woof! Woof!" barked Rufus.
He was always glad to help.

Notes to Grown-ups

Major Themes

Here is a quick guide to the significant themes and concepts at work in *Where's Rufus?*:

- Observation: it's important to notice what's going on around us and to pay attention to obvious signs.
- Family activities: the Plinketts may not have paid enough attention to Rufus's barking at first, but they would not leave for the picnic without him. Everyone, including Rufus, is important to the family.

Step-by-step Ideas for Reading and Talking

Here are some ideas for further give-and-take between grown-ups and children. The following topics encourage creative discussion of *Where's Rufus?* and invite the kind of open-ended response that is consistent with many contemporary approaches to reading, including Whole Language:

- We all know that dogs can't talk. Otherwise, Rufus would simply have told the Plinketts there was a problem instead of having to delay the picnic by hiding. If your child found himself or herself in Rufus's predicament, what would he or she have done? Your child's answer is a key to how he or she would respond to a more serious situation.
- What would your child recommend taking along for a picnic? Have the child describe the ultimate family outing: What kinds of foods would he or she want? What kinds of games would the family play?

Games for Learning

Games and activities can stimulate young readers and

44

listeners alike to find out more about words, numbers, and ideas. Here are more ideas for turning learning into fun:

Woof-Woof Charades
What if, like Rufus, you could only bark and dance around to tell people what you were thinking? To find out how that would feel, and how good you and your child are at communicating without words, play Woof-Woof Charades.

In Woof-Woof Charades, one woof means no, two woofs means yes. Remind your child (and yourself!) that you can only "woof" in this game: NO TALKING! Aside from woofing, you can use any silent acting skills you have to mime the statements suggested below. They are all things the characters in *Where's Rufus?* might say. Write them out on slips of paper, then draw from a hat or bowl and take turns stumping one another for the answers

Woof-Woof words:

- I think it's going to rain!
- You're stepping on my tail.
- I'm hiding in the plant.
- The sun's out now.
- Don't forget the doggie bones!
- Thank you, Rufus!
- I'm flying my kite.
- I hear thunder.
- Let's eat the cake.

Set a timer to put a limit on each person's turn. Encourage your child to refer to the book for clues on how to guess and how to act out the statement on his or her turn.

About the Author
STEPHANIE CALMENSON is the author of many popular books for children. Before turning to writing full-time, she was an elementary school teacher and a children's book editor. Ms. Calmenson lives in New York City.

About the Artist
MAXIE CHAMBLISS creates her spirited pictures in a busy studio in Somerville, Massachusetts. She has been drawing since she was old enough to hold a pencil and now has over twenty children's books to her credit.